ROLF HEIMANN

ROLF'S CORNY COPIA

Featuring Fickle and Fetch

LITTLE HARE

Little Hare Books
8/21 Mary Street, Surry Hills
NSW 2010 AUSTRALIA
www.littleharebooks.com

National Library of Australia
Cataloguing-in-Publication entry

Heimann, Rolf, 1940-
Rolf's corny copia.

1st ed.
For primary school aged children.
ISBN 978 1 92104 967 5.

ISBN 1 921049 67 7.

1. Maze puzzles - Juvenile literature. I. Title.

793.738

Designed by Serious Business
Produced by Phoenix Offset, Hong Kong
Printed in China

5 4 3 2 1

Welcome to *Corny Copia*, my all-new bumper collection of maddening mazes, peculiar puzzles and silly spotter games!

I love corny jokes, and I love corny conundrums even more—and this book is full of both.

As always, my furry friends Fickle and Fetch will join you for the adventure. Together, you'll extinguish a fire, try your hand at birdwatching and egg spotting—as well as take a puzzling parachute ride and solve dozens of mazes and puzzles along the way!

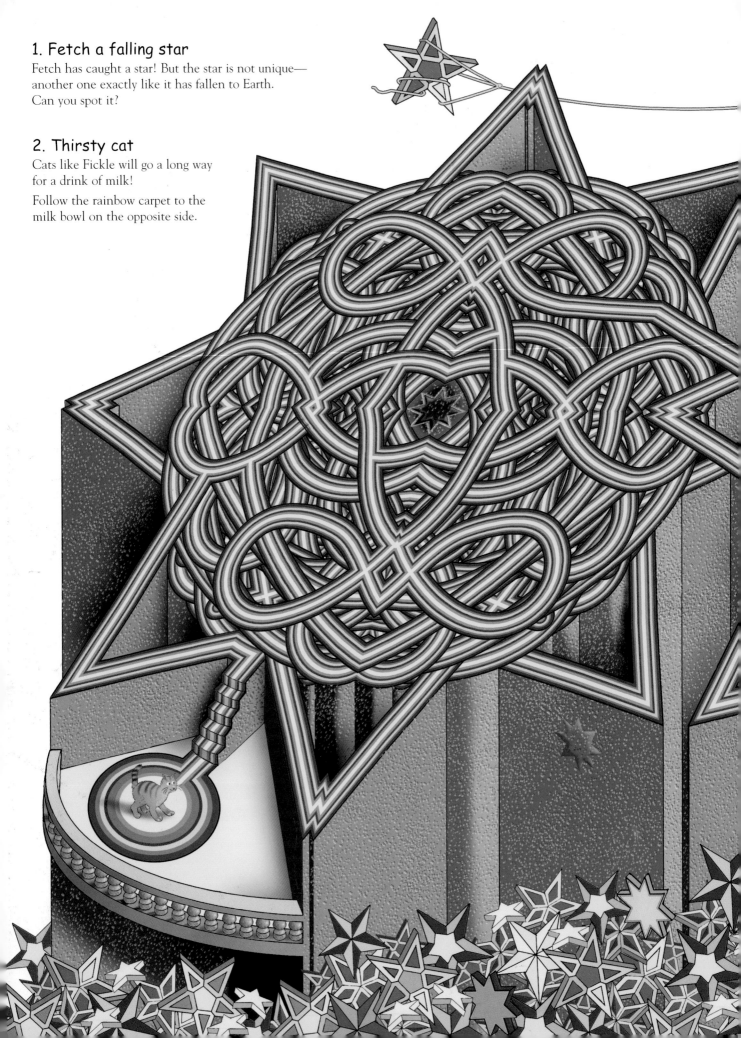

1. Fetch a falling star

Fetch has caught a star! But the star is not unique—another one exactly like it has fallen to Earth. Can you spot it?

2. Thirsty cat

Cats like Fickle will go a long way for a drink of milk!

Follow the rainbow carpet to the milk bowl on the opposite side.

3. Mutant flower

One of the flowers is different from the others. Which one?

4. Hidden shapes

Can you spot these shapes hidden in the picture?

You look for the fish and I'll look for the bone!

5. Tricky truck
Bob the truck driver insists on matching trailers for his road train. Only one of the six trailers matches. Which one?

6. Spaghetti junction
Spaghetti or road? Parsley or trees? What does it matter? Can you make it through this maze in 10 seconds?

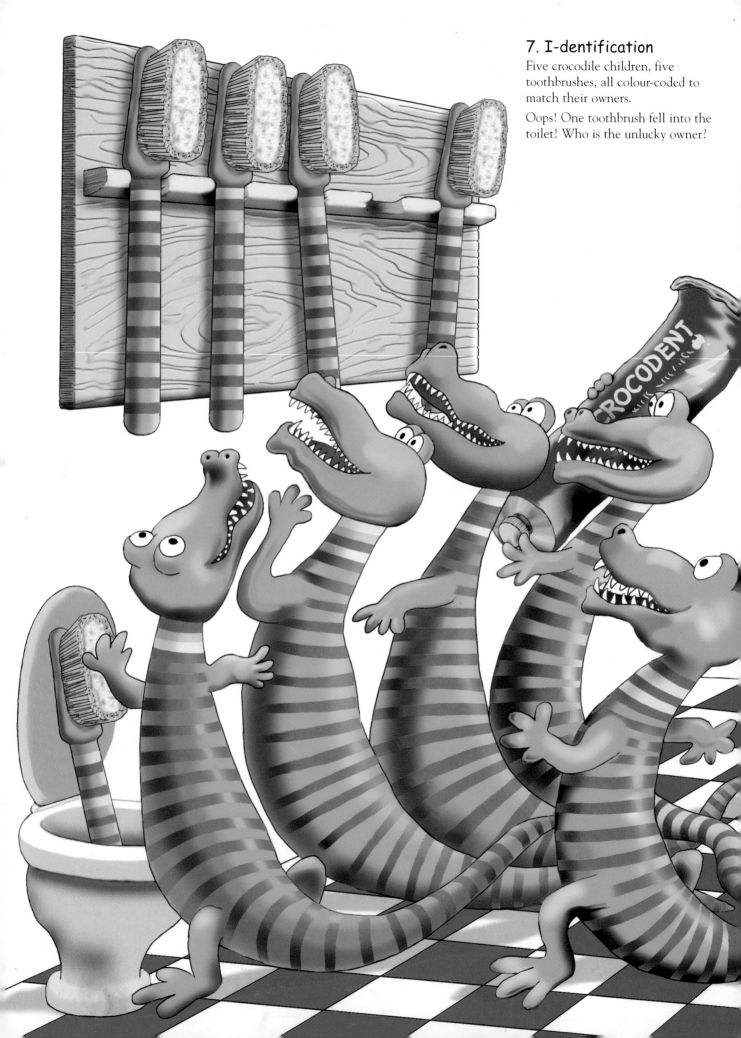

7. I-dentification

Five crocodile children, five toothbrushes, all colour-coded to match their owners.

Oops! One toothbrush fell into the toilet! Who is the unlucky owner?

8. Shortest route

Can you find the shortest route from A to B? It's not so easy!

A

B

Tell that croc to pull his tail from our page!

9. Double destinations

Fetch wants to paddle west to Pelican Lake.

Fickle aims to go north to the waterfall.

Who will have the longer trip?

10. Pelican puzzle

Ten pelicans—all the same. Or are they?
Can you spot the odd one out?

11. Alien barbershop quartet

The aliens sing in beautiful harmony, and luckily they hold up signs with English translations. Which sign should Slork hold up?

12. Get dizzy!

Only one of the eight circles will give you access to the centre without stepping over a black line. Which one?

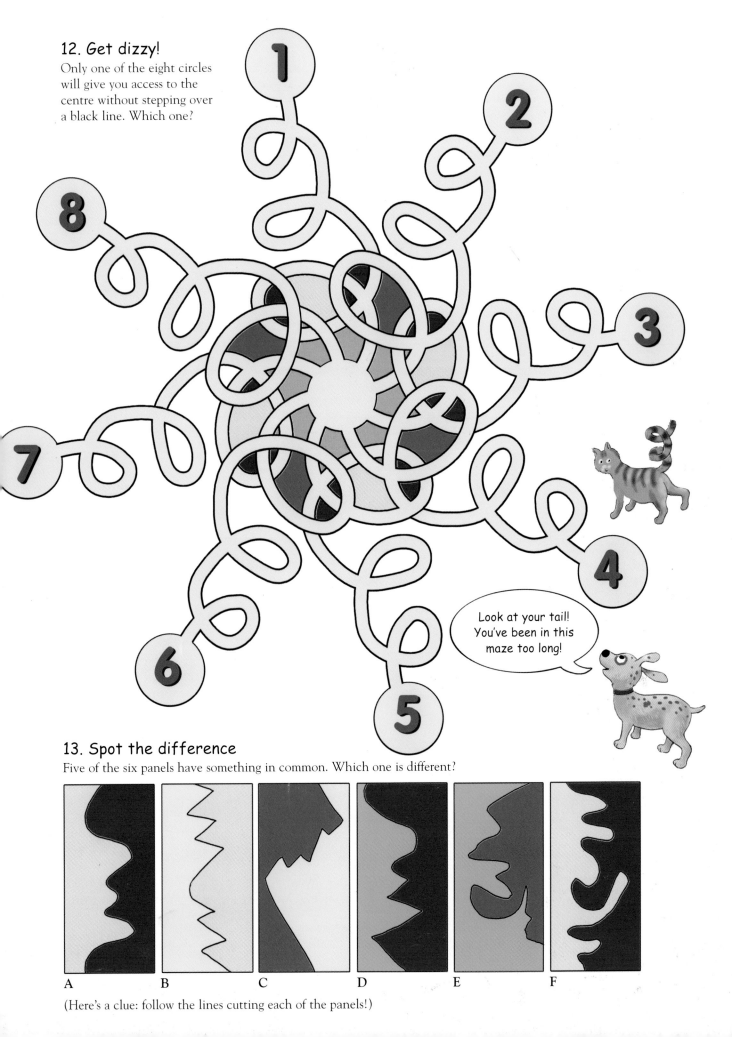

13. Spot the difference

Five of the six panels have something in common. Which one is different?

A   B   C   D   E   F

(Here's a clue: follow the lines cutting each of the panels!)

14. Bridges to Rainbow Island

With so many bridges leading to Rainbow Island it should be easy to find a way across. Well, try it!

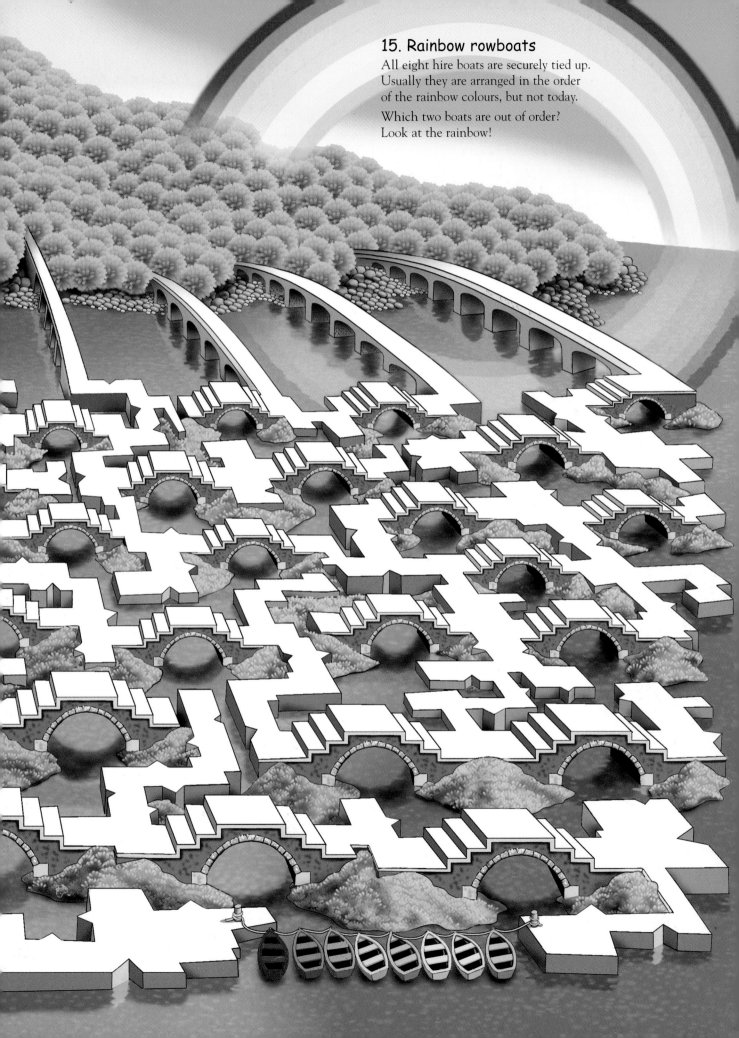

15. Rainbow rowboats

All eight hire boats are securely tied up.
Usually they are arranged in the order
of the rainbow colours, but not today.

Which two boats are out of order?
Look at the rainbow!

16. Emergency!

The fire brigade took 10 minutes to arrive. The police were faster than the ambulance. The ambulance came two minutes after the fire brigade. The television crew arrived after the police but before the fire brigade. Which of the four vehicles came first and which came last?

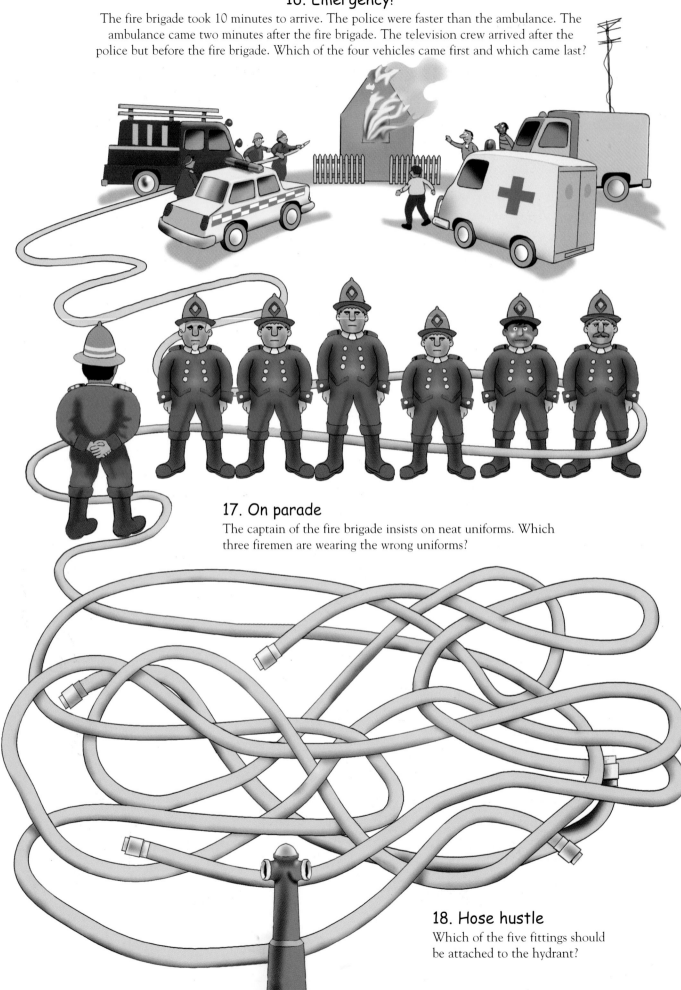

17. On parade

The captain of the fire brigade insists on neat uniforms. Which three firemen are wearing the wrong uniforms?

18. Hose hustle

Which of the five fittings should be attached to the hydrant?

19. Fire!

Find your way to the centre and grab that fire extinguisher!

20. Train trial

What were the railway engineers thinking when they designed Booboo Junction?

The circular sections may look pretty, but they are not even strong enough to hold steam locomotives.

Luckily, they will support the carriages, so it's possible for the trains to pass each other.

Can you work out how?

21. Find these shapes!

Luckily, you have sharp eyes—or do you?

22. Lizards get-together
Can the lizards meet, staying on the white path?

23. Bluebird of speckledness
The speckled bluebird lays its speckled blue eggs anywhere, and not always in the best places. How many eggs are safe from marauding lizards and how many are not?

24. Quick one

Isn't it nice to have an easy one once in a while?

25. Magic mirror

This magic mirror does not like nasty children and shows it by changing their reflection.

Find the 13 things which the mirror has changed.

26. Soup of the day
It should not be too hard to find all the ingredients that the cook requires.

27. Container conundrum
The apprentice has a problem.

How can he measure a litre of water if the only containers are for two and three litres? There is a way!

28. No mix-ups please!
The cook has asked for cold water. Make sure the apprentice is using the hose from the cold tap!

29. Staring at stars

One of these stars is not quite like the others. Which one?

30. Odd one out

Which picture is out of place, and why?

31. Sugar ants

Only one of the nine ants can get to the sugar spoon without stepping over a black line.

32. Stock report
One brother owns ranch W, the other owns ranch XX. They both run sheep and cattle. Each head of cattle is worth $100 and each sheep $50. Which of the brothers has the larger investment?

33. Scenic journey
Is it faster to go by steamer from Black Rock to Red Rock, or from Red Rock to Black Rock?

34. Go with the flow
Which direction does the river flow?

STELLA

BLACK ROCK

35. Outsider:
Which of these 14 items is out of place?

36. Pick the leader
Which of the four donkeys below should lead the group?

37. Reunion

Can you reunite Fetch and Fickle?

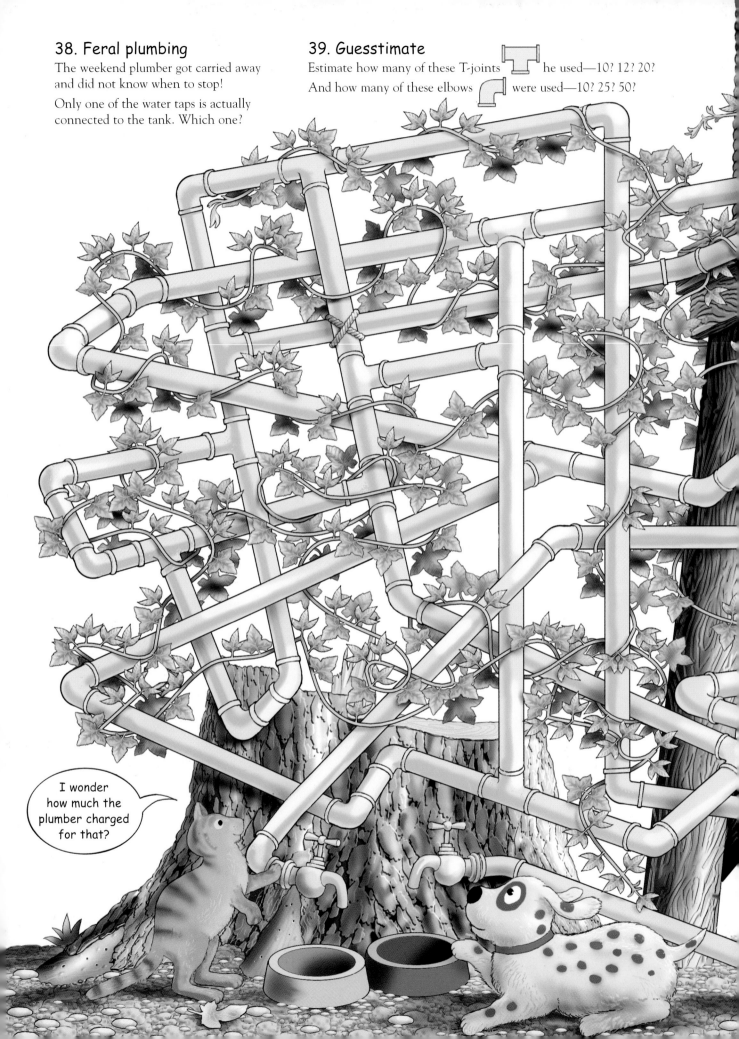

38. Feral plumbing

The weekend plumber got carried away and did not know when to stop!

Only one of the water taps is actually connected to the tank. Which one?

39. Guesstimate

Estimate how many of these T-joints he used—10? 12? 20?

And how many of these elbows were used—10? 25? 50?

I wonder how much the plumber charged for that?

40. Star travel
Find your way to the star.

41. Right label
How should the blue panel be labelled?

42. Facials

Which of the seven faces below completes the sequence?

43. Twin stars

Connect the two stars!

44. Split towers

Fickle could jump the gap, but he decides to be safe and use the path to get to Fetch. So should you!

45. Lost tools

Builders have been working on the towers. They were careless and forgot some of their tools. Can you find them all?

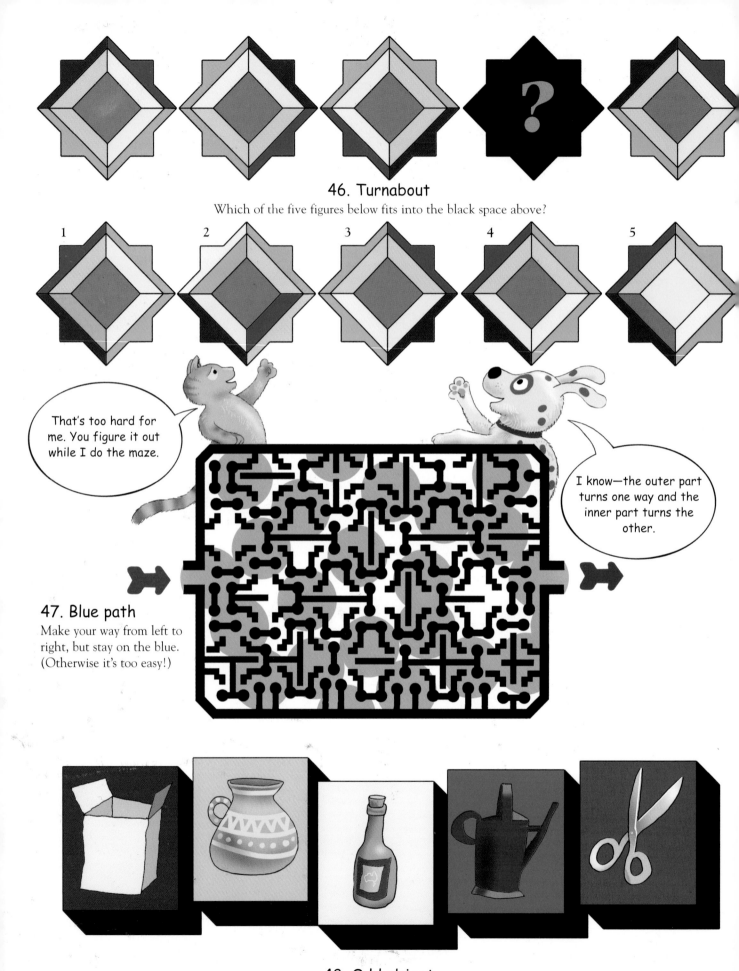

46. Turnabout
Which of the five figures below fits into the black space above?

1   2   3   4   5

47. Blue path
Make your way from left to right, but stay on the blue. (Otherwise it's too easy!)

48. Odd object
Which of these objects doesn't belong?

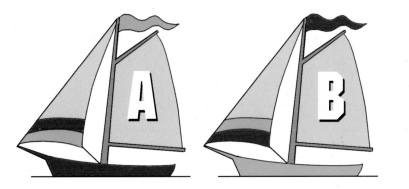

49. Sail away!

Boat A compares to boat B as boat C compares to boat__?

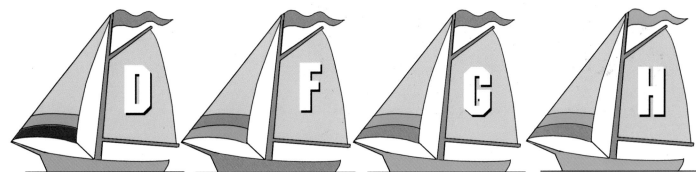

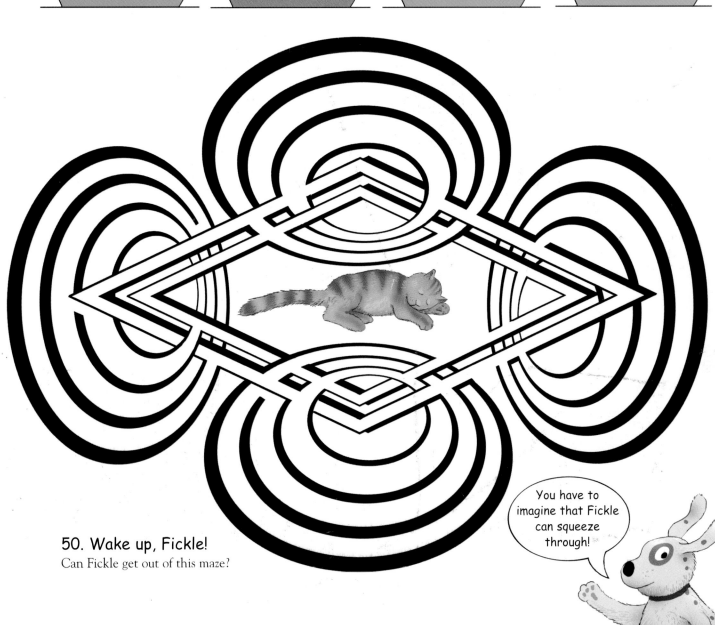

50. Wake up, Fickle!

Can Fickle get out of this maze?

You have to imagine that Fickle can squeeze through!

51. Fowl match

This little island is home to some very unusual birds. Their plumage matches the colour of their eggs.

Nine nests, but only eight birds? One of the parents seems to be late. Which of the eggs is in danger?

52. Foul deed

Some careless anglers have left fishing hooks behind.
Find all 20 hooks before someone gets hurt.

53. Flying squadron
Work out the missing numbers on the blue and the green planes.

54. Up in the air
Fill in the missing numbers on the two balloons on the left.

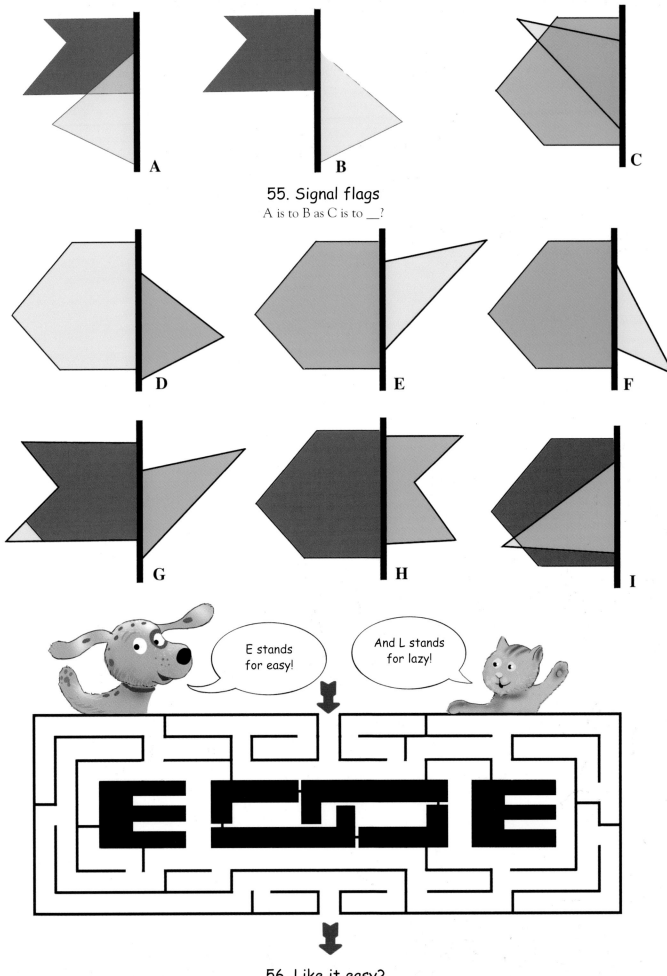

55. Signal flags

A is to B as C is to __?

E stands for easy!

And L stands for lazy!

56. Like it easy?

Then this is the maze for you!

57. Follow the yellow path
Fetch is aiming for the peak with the yellow flag. Help him find the way.

58. Stay on the green
Fickle is aiming for the peak with the green flag. Who will make it to the top first?

59. Birdwatching
How many kinds of birds can you see?

60. Elephantics
All the numbers make sense, if you study them. What number should Tombo have on his side, and which of the seven packets should Rimbo pick up?

Well, that's a load off my shoulders!

61. Have nots
The five things on the bottom row have something that the six things on the top row do not have. What is it?

62. Odd one
Which of the pictures above doesn't belong?

63. Key question
Jack and Jill must have the same set of keys. Which key should go on which key ring to make the two sets of keys identical?

Remember, the colour of the key makes no difference here!

Naturally...

64. Black and white world

It's a long way from the sun to the moon.
There are three ways to get there—
through the clouds, by land or through
the water.

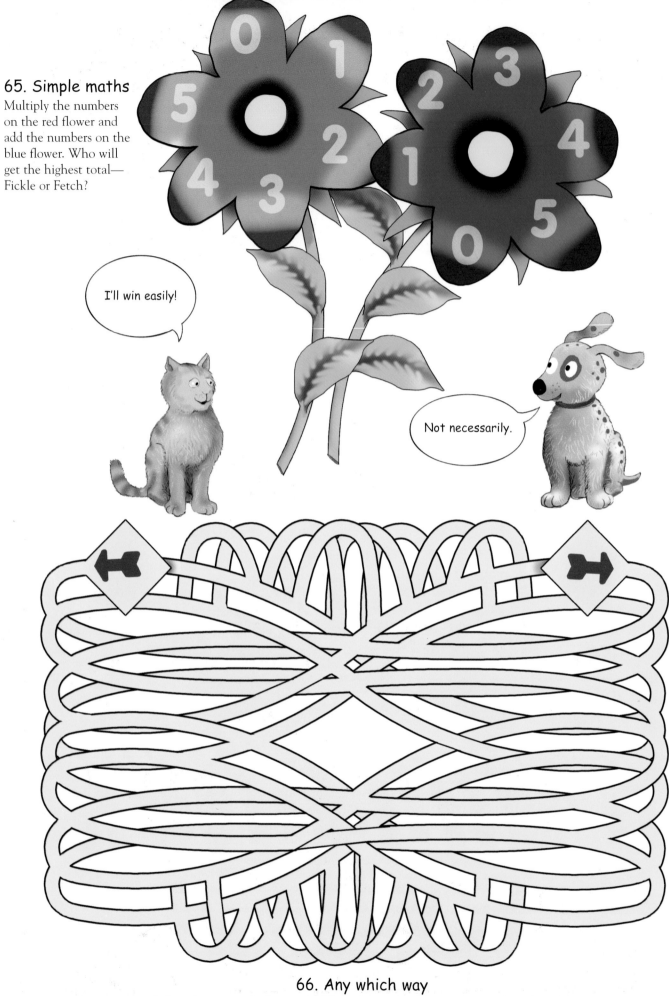

65. Simple maths

Multiply the numbers on the red flower and add the numbers on the blue flower. Who will get the highest total—Fickle or Fetch?

66. Any which way

It doesn't matter which arrow you start from, as long as you get to the other side.

67. It's a breeze-through

And a tight squeeze!

68. Grinning jugs

One of these jugs is broken. Which of the seven jugs below is the right replacement?

69. Maze within a maze

The central maze is closed, but if you're clever you could still find a way in.

70. Plant prices

The red-flowering tree costs twice as much as the white one and $10 more than the yellow one. How much did the seven trees cost altogether?

$100

Closed

Let's go in anyway!

71. Catscan

Once again, it's in one ear and out the other.

72. Dogged pursuit
From ear to ear, or from here to there…

73. Got the blues

Fetch is wearing his favourite blue boots and today he's sticking to the blue path. The sooner he gets to the blue cushion, the sooner he can rest!

74. Red race

Fickle has donned his red boots and he's sticking to the red path. Can Fickle beat Fetch this time?

75. X marks the spot

Or does it? Fetch and Fickle have to land on the right spot so that they can get to the golden door.

Only one of the marked spots will do!

Solutions

1. Fetch a falling star: The matching star is in black.

2. Thirsty cat: The red line shows the path.

3. Mutant flower:
The mutant flower is in black.

4. Hidden shapes:

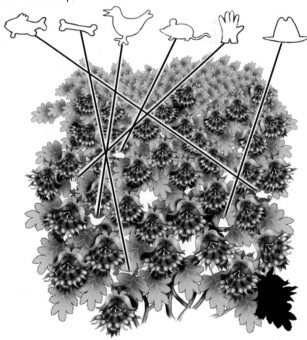

5. Tricky truck: Trailer number 1 matches the truck.

6. Spaghetti junction:
Follow the red line.

7. I-dentification: The middle crocodile is the unlucky owner. (Look at the stripes on the toothbrushes as well as those on their necks.)

8. Shortest route: The black line shows the path through the maze.

9. Double destinations: Fickle will have the longer trip. The way to the waterfall is almost twice as long!

10. Pelican puzzle: The pelican circled in red is different. (Check the black tail.)

11. Alien barbershop quartet:
'Birds sing everywhere' is the translation.

12. Get dizzy!: The red line shows the path through the maze.

13. Spot the difference: Panel E is correct. The dividing line goes from top to bottom, except on panel E.

14. Bridges to Rainbow Island:
Follow the red line.

15. Rainbow rowboats: The two boats in the middle should change places.

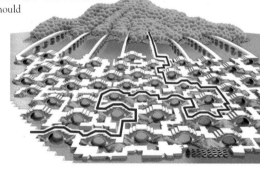

16. Emergency!: The police came first, then the television crew, then the fire brigade and the ambulance last.

17. On parade: The black circles show the differences.

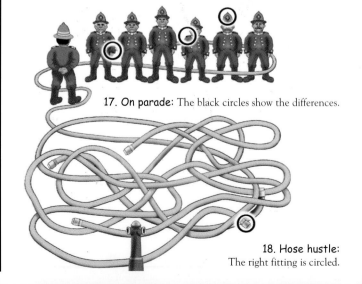

18. Hose hustle:
The right fitting is circled.

19. Fire!: The green line shows the quickest —and only—path through the maze.

20. Train trial: The passenger train has to back up so that the shorter train can go back, as shown below. Now the other train can pass.

21. Find these shapes!: The arrows point to the shapes.

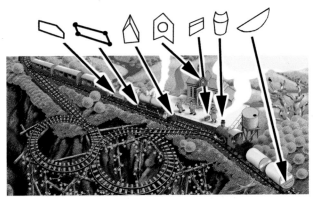

22. Lizards get-together: Follow the red line.

23. Bluebird of speckledness: The safe eggs are circled.

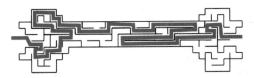

24. A quick one: The red line shows the path.

25. Magic mirror: 13 differences are circled.

26. Soup of the day: The ingredients are circled.

27. Container conundrum: Pour 3 litres of water into the 2 litre container and you're left with 1 litre.

28. No mix-ups please: Follow the red line.

29. Staring at stars: The star in the centre is different.

30. Odd one out: Only the man is certain to crash to earth!

31. Sugar ants: The red line shows the path.

32. Stock report: Ranch XX has the bigger investment. (Ranch W has 18 sheep ($900) and 9 cattle ($900), which amounts to $1800. Ranch XX has 17 sheep ($850) and 11 cattle ($1100), which amounts to $1950.)

33. Scenic journey: It takes half an hour to go from Black Rock to Red Rock and 2 hours from Red Rock to Black Rock.

34. Go with the flow: The steamer takes less time from Black Rock to Red Rock, so the downstream current must be helping.

35. Outsider: The baby, of course! None of the other items can scream.

36. Pick the leader: The donkey on the right. The blanket matches, and the stripes on the hat have changed in the right progression.

37. Reunion: Follow the red line.

38. Feral plumbing: The red line shows the path.

39. Guesstimate: 12 T-joints, 50 elbows.

40. Star travel: The red line shows the path through the maze.

41. Right label: H8.

42. Facials: Face G.

43. Twin stars: Follow the red line.

44. Split towers: The red line shows the way.

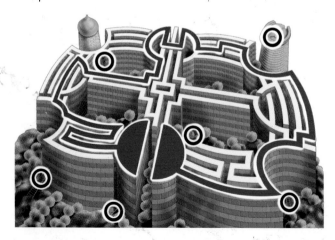

45. Lost tools: The lost tools are circled.

46. Turnabout: The outer frame turns clockwise, while the inner part turns anti-clockwise, so the answer is number 4.

47. Blue path: Follow the red line through the maze.

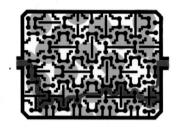

48. Odd object: All the pictures are of containers—except the scissors.

49. Sail away!: The colours are reversed, so the answer is boat G.

50. Wake up, Fickle!: The red line shows the path.

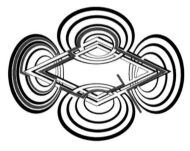

51. Fowl match:

52. Foul deed: The hooks are circled above.

53. Flying squadron: The numbers on the wings add up to the number on the fuselage. The missing numbers are: 8, 8, 8, 8; 20.

54. Up in the air: The number on each balloon follows a pattern of multiplication. The missing numbers are 36 and 5.

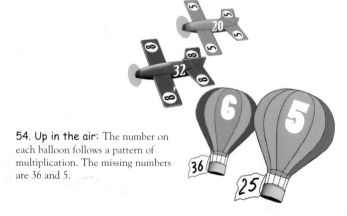

55. Signal flags: Flag E
(The yellow flag is on the other side of the pole.)

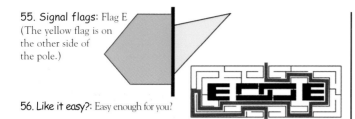

56. Like it easy?: Easy enough for you?

57. Follow the yellow path: The red line shows the path.

58. Stay on the green: Follow the black line.

59. Birdwatching: The lowest bird on the right has a red beak and shorter legs, making it a third kind.

60. Elephantics: The sum of the load is written on the elephants' bodies. The missing number is 11, and the additional load for Rimbo is 9.

61. Have nots: It's legs, of course!

62. Odd one: The number five is always involved—except with the cow.

63. Key question: The blue key goes to Jack, the red one to Jill.

64. Black and white world: The three coloured lines show the paths.

65. Simple maths: Fetch wins with a total of 15. Anything multiplied by 0 equals 0.

66. Any which way:
Follow the red line.

67. It's a breeze-through:
So you don't need help!

68. Grinning jugs: Number 4 is correct.
(Look at the gold tooth and the green stripes on the handles.)

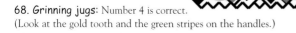

69. Maze within a maze: The black line shows the path.

70. Plant prices: The white tree costs $100, the red one $200 and the yellow one $190. Three red trees = $600, three yellow trees = $570, plus one white tree for $100 makes a total of $1,270.

71. Catscan: The red line shows the path through the maze.

72. Dogged pursuit: Follow the red line.

73. Got the blues: Follow the black line.

74. Red race: The green line shows the path.

75. X marks the spot: Follow the red line to the golden door.

Rolf Heimann was born in Dresden, Germany in 1940. In 1945, he witnessed the total destruction of his home city—which made him a lifelong opponent of war.

At age 18 he migrated to Australia. Over the next few years he worked his way around the country doing all kinds of jobs, including fruit-picking, labouring at railways and working in factories. Every spare hour was spent writing and sketching. Eventually, he settled in Melbourne, where he worked for printers and publishers before finally running his own art studio.

In 1974, Rolf sailed his own boat around the Pacific (and met his future wife, Lila, in Samoa), returning to Australia after two years to concentrate on painting, writing, cartooning and illustrating. He has now published over fifty books, including puzzle and maze books, junior novels and picture books. His books have travelled to dozens of countries and have sold millions of copies around the world.

Also by Rolf Heimann from Little Hare Books:

PUZZLEMAZIA

CRAZY COSMOS

BRAIN BUSTING BONANZA

ASTROMAZE

ZOODIAC

ROLF'S FLUMMOXING FLABBERGASTERS

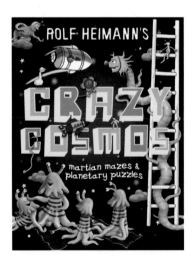

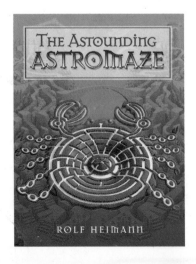